D0120166

This book tells us about a very special garden: The Garden of Life. In this garden you will find the doors to Peace and Love, both internal and external.

The Gardener speaks to the plants and the trees, to the gnomes, the sylphs, the fairies; to the water nymphs and the elves. He reveals to us how even though the bird does not understand the mechanism of flight, nonetheless it flies because it is in its nature to fly, just as it is in man's nature to discover Love.

The Gardener is a book to reflect on and to take pleasure in, a book written from the heart that speaks directly to the heart.

The Gardener

GRIAN

Thorsons
An Imprint of HarperCollins*Publishers*

Thorsons
An Imprint of HarperCollins*Publishers*
77-85 Fulham Palace Road
Hammersmith, London W6 8JB

Originally published 1996 as *El Jardinero* by Ediciones Obelisco.
This edition by Thorsons 1998.

10 9 8 7 6 5 4 3 2 1

A catalogue record for this book
is available from the British Library

ISBN 0 7225 3775 1

Printed and bound in Great Britain by
Caledonian International Book Manufacturing Ltd, Glasgow

Dedication

To Nandy, companion on the path, custodian of the mystery of simplicity.

To Benjamin, eternal navigator of the oceans of life.

To Maria, my mother.

To Harold Sammuli, my beloved Hayo, master of arms in the search for the Holy Grail.

And Our Lady 'La Soterr*ana*', ancestral lady of the sacred lands of Requena.

Contents

The Gardener

Like a red blanket of poppies blossoming in Spring time, the gardener rose from nowhere, wearing leather sandals and carrying a long oak staff.

He wandered through the squares and market, looking for someone who was willing to sell him a spacious piece of land. Eventually he found a place by a sparkling golden stream.

He built a hut and around it a garden, as big as the trails of wind, bordered by ivy, clematis, passionflowers and honeysuckle, and dotted with lilies, violets, irises and pansies.

He sat at the entrance to the garden, offering its peace and beauty to all who wished to take pleasure from it. He told them it was the garden of life, and all those who wished to find peace in it would always find the door open.

Birds and squirrels made their nests in the trees, fairies and elves looked for shelter among its plants, and men found refuge among the flowers.

And the gardener devoted himself to the care of plants and trees, squirrels and birds, fairies, elves and men.

God's Chants

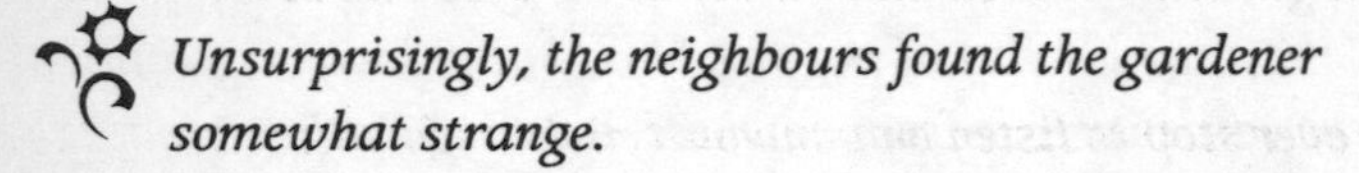

Unsurprisingly, the neighbours found the gardener somewhat strange.

Often they saw him talking to his plants, stroking them and treating them with great affection. And yet he gained no benefit from them, in terms of money or success, and this people found even more strange.

'Why do you stroke your plants and talk to them when they cannot feel your hand or hear you?' one of his neighbours finally asked him.

'And how do you know they cannot feel or hear me?' replied the gardener.

His neighbour was puzzled.

'Well, everybody knows that plants are not able...'

'Nor do most men feel or hear God,' interrupted the gardener, 'yet God does not stop talking and caring for us because of this.'

The neighbour felt increasingly confused, and a little troubled. He asked again:

'And how do you know that God exists? I have never seen him, nor heard him. Nor have I felt him caring for me in the way you speak of.'

The gardener bowed his head sadly and was silent. When the neighbour thought that he was not going to be able to answer him, the gardener looked him kindly in the eyes and said:

'If you ever stop to listen on a moonlit night, you will only realise that the crickets sing when they keep quiet; it is the silence that warns you of the presence of that hidden life. God has never stopped singing, he has never stopped talking to us and caring for us, and it is for that reason that most men do not notice his love.

'If God stopped singing, even if you realized the very next instant that he was there, it would be too late.'

And, smiling, he added:

'But do not worry, God will never stop singing.'

'Then you will never be able to convince us that God exists,' the neighbour answered with a triumphant smile.

The gardener started to laugh, and putting a hand on his neighbour's shoulder, he told him:

'Just as it is with the crickets... If you can find internal peace, the silence will reveal to you God's chants.'

When the Leaves Fall

'Gardener,' called the girl from the garden fence.

'Why do some trees lose their leaves in winter, while others protect themselves from the cold with the same summer leaves?'

'Why do you wash your face each morning in The Looking Glass Spring?'

'Why do you arrange your ribbon before the mirror each day when the sun shines through your window?'

The gardener fell silent while the girl observed him with an innocent look of surprise.

'The water with which you wash your face in the morning is different each day,' the gardener continued.

'I don't understand, sir.'

The gardener went over to the fence and, pointing to the trees in the garden, said to the girl:

'There is not a tree that doesn't lose its leaves. Some strip their yawning branches each autumn. Others drop their leaves little by little all through the year, while new leaves come out and

take the place of the old ones. That's why it seems to you that they don't lose their green attire.'

'Wouldn't it be easier to always have the same leaves without having to change them each time?' asked the girl, while looking at the oak tree nearby.

'Doesn't your mother make you new dresses each spring so that you will look more beautiful and you can stop wearing the old ones?'

'Yes,' answered the girl, looking him in the eyes.

'And when a dress becomes old, what does your mother do with it?'

'She makes it into rags or scraps to make bedspreads for my bed.'

'Well, think about it. The trees make a quilt around themselves with the old leaves from the trees, that will nourish the ground from where they will later take their sustenance and that gives life to other plants and animals.'

An expression of happy astonishment came upon the girl's face.

'The trees know a lot, gardener!'

The innocence of the girl's eyes sent a rush of energy up and down his back.

'Be, then, wise like the trees and when life asks you to drop the old leaves from your mind and heart, have no doubts. That way your soul can have a new dress available each spring.'

The Weed

On one occasion, the gardener was preparing to remove a weed that was growing right beside one of the most special plants in the garden, when he seemed to hear something similar to a voice inside the weed that said:

'No, please don't pull me out! Let me carry on living!'

The gardener was confused; he stopped, and opened his eyes in surprise.

'Perhaps my imagination is playing tricks on me. Or perhaps this plant has something to show me,' he thought, while watching the weed with astonishment.

'If I talk to my trees and plants, why should they not talk to me?' he asked himself in a quiet voice.

So, he decided not to remove the weed even though, in time, it would grow until its leaves completely covered the prized plant.

One afternoon in May, a violent tempest unleashed itself, and a strong hailstorm ruined a large part of the garden. After the storm was over the gardener walked around amongst deformed flowers and torn leaves, grumbling with resignation about what had happened.

He nearly did not dare look when he arrived at the place where the prized plant was to be found. But, to his surprise, it was still intact, while the weed that covered it lay ruined at his feet.

The gardener looked with tenderness at the weed that he had tried to pull out, and thinking it over to himself, said in a low voice:

'Sometimes what appears to be ugly, inharmonious and perverse performs wonderful tasks that the most beautiful of creatures would never be capable of.'

The Most Beautiful Flower

'I see that you are sad and thoughtful,' the gardener said to the silent girl.

She looked at him with lifeless eyes and without answering dropped her head again.

'What has happened today to make you so gloomy? Every day you come to my garden in the late afternoon and every afternoon you change into the most tender and sweet-scented flower...'

'I'm not a beautiful flower,' the girl interrupted.

The gardener fell silent.

'Today I have seen my image in the Mirror Lake,' she went on, without lifting her head. 'At last I've become a woman, but I do not possess the beauty that I had dreamed of so much.'

The gardener now understood.

'Everybody says that roses are the most beautiful flowers. And indeed they are!' he asserted, while the girl turned her face towards him. 'However, I like the little verbena that grows at the foot of the rose, and I enjoy gazing upon the mischievous pansies, and the elongated and introverted tulips, and a field of daisies wild under the sun.'

'Do you mean, gardener, that there is more beauty in the verbena than in the roses?'

The gardener looked towards the evening sky.

'I mean that beauty is not really in this or that flower more than it is here or there. Beauty is in the look that beholds it. If the look is alert enough, it will find the goddess of beauty wherever it looks, because she gave light to everything that exists.

'If you still wish to be more beautiful and to become an image of the goddess on earth, look towards the sky and ponder the big clouds that sail majestically across the blue. Look closely at those perfectly rounded, shiny cotton clouds, and see how their beauty pales beside the other clouds that have been perforated by the winds, and that let the sun's rays pass through.'

The gardener fell silent while looking intently towards the girl, who was now watching the clouds.

'Let the light from your soul shine through the pores of your skin, and the whole world will see in you the most radiant Beauty.'

From The Love of Trees

The arrival of autumn began to announce itself in the garden. The oaks and the maples had slowly begun to strip themselves, dropping a leaf here and there on the green lawn surrounding the pond.

A young couple, who used to visit the solitude of the garden to find calm, went to see the gardener.

'Forgive us for bothering you, gardener, but we consider you to be wise and good and we would like you to give us some advice on the new life my beloved and I are going to begin. Very soon we will join our lives in matrimony, and we would be grateful if you could tell us how we must nurture our love so that in time it doesn't wither.'

'Nobody is wise and good,' answered the gardener with a smile. 'Wisdom and goodness are like a hole in the ground; the bigger it is, the emptier you find it. But, as you have asked for my advice, I will tell you what Life has shown me. Sometimes by hard lessons, and other times with a caress.'

Inviting them to sit down on the grass, he told them: 'Be careful that your love is not like that the mistletoe has for the oak, sinking its roots in its trunk to suck its sap and strength. Nor let it be like the love of bramble for the pine shoot, growing and wrapping around it and suffocating it between its spines.

'Rather, aim for a love like that of the trees. Each one embraces the earth with its own roots, and rises up in the morning sun with arms stretched towards the sky, giving thanks for each new dawn.

'Take care to plant your roots at a sufficient distance from each other, in case the branches of one make the other's flee, and it has to twist its trunk and cannot grow towards the clouds.

'Be careful that you keep the correct distance, so that the earth can sufficiently dampen your roots and the wind can clean the dry leaves from the branches. So that you can grow a large and sturdy crown to give shade to travellers and nests for the birds in the sky, and so that when you have grown and scattered your seeds to the wind, the ends of your branches will touch one another in the high reaches, and you can rejoice at the sound of the Dance of Life.'

The Mystery of Life

In the midst of the warm peace of summer, the woodland decorated its soul with a framework of bright light, created by the sun in its attempt to break through the thickness of the forest.

The warmth, sensitive as a friend's hand on the shoulder, seemed to invite the gardener to rest in the shady place by the spring.

All his effort and hard work was now behind him. The meaning that had led his life up until that moment was stretched out at the end of his summer nap; and the sum of his successes and failures vanished like a butterfly in the thickness of the forest.

With a gaze of peace and tranquillity and a naked heart, the gardener leant back on the trunk of an elm tree, drawing in the breath of the forest among the ferns.

In a moment that seemed eternal, the seed of a pine tree threw itself from the tree that gave it life and fell swirling towards a shady spot on the fertile ground.

Two trembling tears appeared in the gardener's eyes, and in a quiet voice he said to the tree:

'Thank you, brother pine tree, for showing me the deepest mystery of Life.'

The Fairy Crown

On mild nights, the gardener liked to go for slow walks along the garden paths.

One night, when the moon was reflecting itself in the pond, the gardener saw a faint light among the azaleas. He approached, and parted the plants that were preventing him seeing the source of the light, where he met with a tiny fairy moving to and fro among the flowers.

On hearing the rustling of leaves, the fairy turned to face him.

'Hello, gardener,' she said.

And turning her back on him, she continued what she was doing.

'Who are you?' the gardener asked softly.

The fairy turned around again, and somewhat impatiently answered:

'A fairy, can't you see?'

And then continued with her task.

The gardener stayed to watch the slender figure of the fairy, with her dragonfly wings and her hair long and black as night, while she fluttered back and forth among the azaleas.

'And what are you doing?' he finally plucked up the courage to ask.

'I'm looking for my crown of golden pollen,' she answered without a pause.

'I lost it this morning while I was painting these flowers and I don't know where it could have fallen.'

'Let me help you,' the gardener said.

And getting down on all fours, he carefully crawled into the bushes. Pushing aside the grass and pebbles with the tips of his fingers, at last he found a golden, effervescent, ring-sized hoop.

'Is this it?' he said, afraid to touch it in case it came apart in his hands.

'Yes!' answered the fairy, jumping up and down with joy.

With a quick flutter she threw herself on the crown, and with a delicate gesture she set it on her head.

'Thank you, gardener!'

'Oh! It's nothing,' he said, a little confused.

Without giving him time to understand what was happening, the fairy darted up to face him and, with exquisite sweetness, planted a kiss on his nose. She looked at him briefly and then disappeared, fluttering among the garden foliage.

The gardener sat a long time on the ground trying to understand what had happened.

The next day everybody in the village was talking about the golden gleam of the gardener's nose.

The Monk

A monk arrived at the garden at the time when autumn afternoons colour the horizon red.

Without saying a word he settled into the gardener's hut, and there they stayed for three days and three nights, sharing bread, the work in the garden, and the late afternoons by the old oak at the spring.

Not a word was said between them, only warm and friendly looks and one or two pats on the back.

When the monk left, they shook hands, and without a word they promised each other friendship for ever.

The Little Plant

A man who used to seek solace in the garden, once told him:

'Gardener, I have often seen you working with these plants that you are now caring for with such adoration. From what I can see these must be your favourite plants, as you give them so much love and affection.'

The gardener gave him a kindly look.

'Because you have seen me give so much time to these plants does not mean that they are my favourites. The truth is that all the plants and trees in my garden are in my heart. What happens is that each plant and tree requires a different amount of time, according to its growth and needs.'

'But there must be one plant that is your favourite,' the man insisted.

'Well... it's true that there is a plant that I feel something special for,' the gardener said, lowering his head.

'Could you show me which one, gardener?'

'It's a small plant with white flowers that is found beside the door of my hut,' answered the gardener.

'You know, I often come to your garden, but I have never seen you care for that plant,' said the man with a puzzled gesture.

The gardener gave a hint of a smile.

'There are plants that need more caring than others. When a plant grows in an ungainly fashion, and has no flowers, one has to prune and feed it. When a tree grows twisted, one has to straighten it with a stake. But when a plant gives the best it's got it is not necessary to do anything, other than leave it to grow and cover itself with flowers. That is how my little plant by the hut is.

'When I come out to sit in the door of my hut on summer nights, I speak to it; and I tell it my hopes and wishes, disappointments and troubles, my feelings and dreams. And it understands me in the twinkle of its small flowers, and it soothes me with the scent of its perfume. And when I go in or out of my hut, whenever I leave or return, it is always waiting to say goodbye, or to welcome me.'

And inviting the man to walk round the garden paths with him, the gardener said:

'All the trees and plants in my garden are in my heart, but only my little plant by the hut knows my soul.'

The Chant of Love

The gardener submerged his spirit in the solitude of the pond, and the twilight of that April afternoon inspired his soul to compose a sweet melody:

'Oh, God. Beloved Life. Warm breeze of light that scatters the sad groans of my soul. Unfathomable love that opens the lips of my heart to the golden splendour of your sweetness.

'Let me feel again the divine warmth of your words on my heart, the soft caress of your smile before my eyes.

'Embrace me in your arms so I can lose myself in your heart, and disappear in the bottomless depths of your presence; far away from the heartbreaking deception of separation, away from the pitiful cries of the discarded soul.

'Oh, God. My Love. My Life. What a long path that leads to your throne! How cruel the sweet wound of your calling in my heart, of your memory in everything I see!

'Oh, God... My Soul... My Life.'

The twilight sweetly covered the gardener's back with its cloak of purple, and the first star of the night dressed its tears with silver sparkles. Through the sky the night spread its garlands of light, and the birds, silent in their nests, listened to the soft voice of the gardener singing his prayer among the poplar trees.

'Sweet Beloved...

'I would like to be like the oak, firm on the ground, so that my feet are never weakened along the path.

'I would like to be patient like the olive tree, so that the new stems of life could be reborn from my old and rough soul.

'I would like to have the knowledge of the old evergreen oak, the one with the high branches that looks at the still dawn to know your silent paths.

'I would like to be like the generous almond tree, offering its flowers on the bare and dried up bark, and enjoy the delight of the cherry tree that calls the birds in the distance so that they come and eat its fruit.

'I would like to have the singing voice of the poplar and the gratefulness of the birch that raises its white hands to the sky, so it can keep singing in tune to your praises.

'I would like to be humble like the violets, and pure like the beautiful roses.

'I would like to be simple like the daisies and fertile like the field of wheat, so I could cover the earth with the light of your Love.

'But it has been your will that I should be a simple man, and as I cannot now aspire to be more than what you wanted for me, teach me at least to accept myself as a simple human being, and let me embrace myself at your feet, as the ivy embraces the oak's trunk, so that I can immerse myself in the jasmine scent of your presence.'

The Fiesta

One night, an elf of average height appeared in front of the gardener, jumping from the branches of a walnut tree.

'Hello, gardener,' he said with a broad smile. 'I come as a messenger of the spirits of nature of this region, to ask you to join us in the party we will have tomorrow night in this garden.'

Once he had recovered from the surprise of such an unexpected appearance, the gardener said to the elf:

'I am very aware of the work you have been doing throughout the spring. More flowers than ever, with the most beautiful colours, have blossomed everywhere, and in all the trees I've seen lots of young shoots that are continuing to grow strong and beautiful. It's good to celebrate the end of your efforts with a big party. Although, I don't see how a human being is going to fit into your festivities and revelry.'

'Well,' said the elf, tilting his head, 'it's true we never invite humans to our celebrations, because man doesn't respect our work or the life that surrounds him. But you are different; you help us in our labours, and we'd like you to join us now that we have finished our work.'

The gardener thought for a moment about his words while the elf was waiting for an answer.

'All right...' he said at last. 'Tomorrow night I will join you in your celebration.'

And the elf, giving a little jump of joy, disappeared among the garden's foliage.

'See you tomorrow, gardener,' he heard a voice say as he went away.

The following night, all the spirits of nature from the surrounding region turned out in the garden: gnomes, sylphs, water nymphs and elves, tiny fairies and mischievous imps. And the gardener joined them in their celebration, singing and dancing until dawn.

Some days later, a shepherd said that he had seen the gardener dancing alone among the ash trees and the honeysuckle on the night of Saint John.

The Transformation

A young man with splendid ideas, who often asked the gardener for advice, went to his hut one cold, rainy night.

As though he had been awaiting his visit, the gardener beckoned him to enter as he opened the door. He helped him to take off his wet coat and asked him to sit down by the fire.

When he had warmed his hands a little, the young man asked: 'Good friend, I feel a deep uneasiness in my heart. Since I have left my boyhood behind and started to think like a man, I have been observing the world around me, and I have found good and great things among human beings and nature. But, each time I've found other things that tear my soul and make me sad. I've seen that in the world there is injustice and a lack of kindness, I've seen hopelessness in the eyes of the poor and the ill, I've seen the claws of greed clutched in the hearts of men and the mists of hate clouding the reasoning and justice between brothers. And each time I see these things my confused heart cries out and my soul shouts to the heavens, looking for an answer to so much unhappiness. And I think I'd like to change this world, so that everybody could live in joy and harmony. But what can one man do against so much grief and devastation?'

The young man fell silent, hiding his face between his hands.

'You can change the world,' said the gardener in a soft tone of voice.

'How can one man change the world?' the young man asked.

'By changing oneself,' was the gardener's reply.

'I don't understand. If only one man changes, how can mankind change?'

'Each human being is the entire human race, his image shooting towards the ardent depths of the cosmos,' said the gardener, looking into the fire. 'When a human being submerges himself into the ocean of Light, all human beings are caught by the brilliance of his goodness.'

'I still don't understand,' said the boy quite innocently.

'You don't have to understand. Birds do not understand the mechanisms of flight; however, they fly. It is as natural for them to fly as it is natural for a human to attain Love.'

The fire crackled intensely on the gardener's last word, and both men kept quiet for an instance, captivated by the dancing flames in the fireplace.

The young man looked at the gardener and in doubt looked at the flames again. He turned his head and looked at the gardener once more and at last made up his mind.

'And what must I do to change myself?'

'Not try to,' answered the gardener with a smile.

A look of astonishment came over the boy's face, and he couldn't utter a single word.

'If you don't try you won't achieve it,' continued the gardener. 'You have to wish for the change within yourself and be open so that the transformation takes place inside you. But if you try to provoke it, a conflict will begin in your heart that will leave you wounded and hurt. Simply open your heart and let the transformation take place when Life considers it the right moment.

'The bird isn't shown how it should fly. Nobody explains to the fish how it must swim. Clearly, one day they throw themselves to the wind and to the sea, and their own nature does the rest.

'To love is written in man's nature, a love as big as the ocean, a love which covers everything. Man has only to throw himself to the tides of Life with an open heart and his own nature will do the rest.

'It is Love that will bring about the transformation in your soul and with it will come the transformation of the world.'

And absorbed in his thoughts, the gardener finished by saying in a quiet voice:

'When a human being finds Love, the whole universe shudders in its splendour.'

The Looking Glass Spring

'Why do you call the source of water that you have in your garden "The Looking Glass Spring"?' the woman asked the gardener.

'So that when you drink from it you look at yourselves in the mirror of its depths,' the gardener replied.

'And why do you want us to look at our reflection in the water?'

'So that you can see the truth,' was the man's simple answer.

'I don't understand what you are trying to tell me, gardener.'

The gardener let a smile slip from his lips.

'By calling it "The Looking Glass Spring" I'm encouraging you to search for your gaze upon the surface of the depths, and when you find your eyes in the water, framed by the clouds in the sky, you'll find yourselves one step from seeing the truth of your existence.'

'Well, I've looked at myself in the spring many times but I've seen nothing of what you say,' the woman told him, confused.

'Take a good look at yourself. A good look,' answered the gardener tenderly.

The Best of Life

A trader went to see the gardener while he was resting at the hut door.

'Good afternoon, gardener,' he said. 'I've come to offer you a business deal that's going to interest you for sure.'

And seeing the passiveness of the gardener, he began to tell him about an arrangement he had thought of that could be advantageous to both of them, an arrangement in which the gardener would promise to cultivate a large expanse of land exclusively of roses so that, later, the trader could sell them in the town's market.

'Gardener, with your green fingers our roses will be the best in town,' concluded the trader with a satisfied gesture.

'Thanks, but I'm not interested,' said the gardener with his usual smile.

'But you could earn a lot of money... ' claimed the merchant, surprised.

'I'm not interested in the money.'

'But everybody is interested in money... '

'Not me.'

'How can you say that? Money is necessary to survive... '

'Oh, well... ! I eat and sleep every day, I have clothes to wear and a hut that gives me refuge on winter nights,' said the gardener calmly.

The trader could not believe that the gardener had rejected his offer.

'And also...' he insisted, 'you would be doing the work you like, gardener.'

'I already do the work I like.'

'But... '

The trader was left with his mouth open. Then he closed it, stood up and left the garden, saying between his teeth as he left, 'I'll never understand those who stubbornly insist on living in poverty and missing out on the best of life.'

The gardener spent the afternoon listening to the musical sounds of the birds and contemplating the wonderful sunset that the universe offered.

The Strange Look

Many of the people who passed often through the garden talked about the gardener's eyes. They saw that at certain moments his look changed; it became as profound as the immensity of the cosmos, and through it you seemed to see the stars of the firmament.

One day, some women from the town, who usually brought him milk and flour, pointed out the strangeness of that look to the gardener.

'Oh... well... ' he stammered, a little disturbed, 'I have been told about it on several occasions.'

And he fell silent, without knowing how to explain what he felt when the expression of his eyes changed.

One of the women persisted:

'It's always been said that the eyes are the mirror of the soul, and if this is so, in your look can be seen a big and beautiful soul. Your look... '

'That look is not mine,' he interrupted.

The women were confused at the unexpectedness of his statement.

The gardener, now calmer, lowered his head, trying to find the words that would let him explain how he felt when it happened.

'It's so difficult to explain but... ' he blurted out after a moment. 'There are times when I suddenly feel as if someone much bigger and more perfect than me is softly taking over my hands and lips, and then I become a silent spectator, watching what that being does or says through me. And I feel a great peace infuse me, and I enjoy gazing at the perfection of his gestures and the pureness of his words. I also feel that through my eyes he radiates all his love and sweetness, and I realize that his words reach to the deepest heart of all those with whom he speaks.

'That is what happens when you see my look change. The truth is, it's not me who looks at you through my eyes, but someone sublime and perfect, who, captivated, I observe, and who I love in my dearest heart.'

From that day on the women stopped going to the hut to take him milk and flour.

The Treasure

Nobody knew what the gardener's life had been like up to the day he appeared looking for land on which to create his garden. He had never spoken to anybody about his past, his family, or of any of the places he had seen.

One morning, a neighbour and friend of the gardener asked him:

'What was your life like before you arrived here? You've never spoken about it, and I imagine that, as in anybody's life, you will have had wonderful moments that sometimes you are happy to remember.'

The gardener lowered his head, and his face lit up with a smile that is born from beautiful, lived-through memories.

'The past is an illusion that we keep in our hearts, in the same way as the wine producer keeps his best wine, waiting for the occasion that is special enough to be worthy of its savour, but that somehow never seems to arrive as the years pass.

'Perhaps this is that special occasion. One that comes from the hand of those hearts joined by friendship.'

The gardener's friend smiled with a grateful gesture; meanwhile the gardener invited him to take a long walk in the garden.

'Many years ago, I left the land in which I lived with my family and friends, and travelled all over the world looking for the biggest treasure any human could ever lay his eyes on. I walked through green, grass-covered countryside and majestic high mountains. I sank my feet in the desert sand and washed my face in the waves of all the seas. And looking for my treasure I experienced fear, anguish and loneliness. I journeyed into the heart of life, scanning its horizons until at last I came upon the castle battlements where so much that I yearned for was hidden. I opened the doors, saw the treasure and returned, without knowing why I hadn't kept it in my knapsack.

'After that I kept on walking, going from place to place in no fixed direction, until finally I understood that the treasure had just been the excuse for my journey; that the pure and eloquent soul was to be found in the succession of my footprints in the sand. And my steps, and with those my treasure, brought me to this place, where I decided to give life to what the path had shown me.

'That is why I created this garden - the living embodiment of an unobtainable treasure, and one that is always mine.'

The two men remained silent for a long time, while they contemplated the agile games of the dragonflies, jumping over the polished surface of the spring water.

'And your friends?' asked the gardener's friend, breaking the silence. 'Having known as many lands as you have, I suppose you have made many friends on your way?'

'Oh, yes! Many friends!' answered the gardener. 'Wonderful friends, whom I loved to an ecstasy of tenderness deep in my heart.

'Some hurt me when our paths separated. Perhaps I didn't know how to understand them. Who knows. One day, somebody appears on your path and you share with him your life, your hopes, your joys, doubts and memories; and for a time your mutual devotion creates a crystal palace where the spirits of love dance and play. Later, the day arrives when the paths of both your lives part ways, and with the look of a hurt soul, your arms reach out, trying to touch once more the tips of his fingers in the void.

'Perhaps one day your paths will meet again, and the spirits of love will dance again in their silver palace. Perhaps his footprints will never be found again and the image of a friend in the distance reminds me of the enchantment of past days.

'But, anyhow, my beloved friends are always with me. I often meet them in the fertile plains of my imagination; and I speak to them again about my hopes and doubts, and they listen to me with the love that flowers from their hearts. And together we plan new adventures, new journeys on the paths of the tireless souls, and we unite again in an embrace, so that our hearts become one in union in the immense tapestry of the stars.'

The gardener rested his gaze on the horizon, as if in the distance he found all his friends again on the long path. And from his lips his soul broke out in a whisper:

'My friends... My path... My treasure...'

The Spirit of the Wind

With the arrival of the Autumn, the wind began to whip across the land of the region. The dry leaves performed their ritual dances in the streams in the hills, and the bare layers of red earth wove scarlet embroideries into the radiant sunsets.

The gardener took up his forgotten stick again and set out on the path that led to the top of the highest mountain in the area. This mountain was like a huge dragon lying on its paunch, the scene of more battles with the elements than the scars on its skin could reveal and the repository of more knowledge than its appearance made one suspect.

Between its ridges, thought the gardener, he could find the sweet silence of solitude. He was there three days and three nights, sheltered from the spirit of the mountain, talking with the stubborn muteness of his Maker.

And on the third day the spirit of the wind came and spoke with him. As big as two men, the wind's eyes conveyed the sweet peace of angelic beings.

'Good morning, gardener,' it whispered into his soul. 'The spirits of the forests of this region have told me a lot about you. And my curiosity has led me to look for you for the last three days, and at last I have found you here.'

'Good morning, mighty friend of the plains,' answered the gardener. 'God knows I was not expecting such an agreeable visitor. But I must tell you that it would please me very much to have a long chat with you.'

And making a kind gesture with his hand, he said:

'Please, sit down here with me and grant the spirit of the mountain and I the grace of sharing the wisdom that your long journeys have offered you.'

And the spirit of the wind, placing the blue transparency of his body on a nearby rock, said to the gardener:

'We have a lot to tell each other. Let me rest here with you for a few days, while my sylphs go over the region.'

The three of them were there together while the full moon lasted, talking about lands and men, fairies and angels, stormy seas and sacred mountains... before the watchful and silent presence of Him who created them.

The Two Masks

Hearing of the gardener's fame, a stranger arrived in town. On his way to find the garden, he noticed the attitude of his neighbours towards the gardener was very different. Some warned the stranger that it would be better not to meet the gardener, that he was a man with strange and dangerous ideas, and that his influence could be harmful to those who did not have sufficient spiritual strength. Others said that the gardener was a kind-hearted being and a saint, as wise as an ancient King, and so pure that evil was unthinkable in him.

When the stranger at last found the gardener, he told him what the town had said about him.

'Who is telling the truth?' he finished by asking. 'Those who say you're dangerous and wicked, or those who say you're a present-day saint?'

'Neither one nor the other,' was the gardener's simple reply. 'I'm neither a saint nor a villain. I'm simply one more man.'

'But how can you explain the fact that you stir up such conflicting passions among your neighbours?' the stranger asked.

The gardener smiled wearily.

'Everyone sees things through the filter of their fears and anxieties, of their hopes and doubts.

'My words appear dangerous to those who do not want to be disturbed from their dreams, to those who are afraid to wake up and realize that life is different from how they always thought. They know that if they listen to what comes out of my mouths with an open heart, they will feel obliged by their souls to change the direction of their lives to a degree that they are not willing to accept. And for this reason, to justify their fear and blindness, they keep me away from their lives with blame and rejection.

'For others, my words are a song of hope in the darkness of their lives, but a song which, deep down, they believe they cannot sing. That's why they justify their idleness by saying that only saints can be like that, and not a mere mortal.

'There are others still who do not dare to walk alone in life, but in the same way as a shipwrecked person grasps a piece of wood, they grasp onto whoever is shown a door towards the light, in the hope that another can release them from their pain and suffering, not realising that nobody can make the journey for them, they can only show them the way.

'For this reason some see in me a danger, others a saint, and others their personal driftwood of salvation. And none of them are able to see the truth.'

'And what is the truth, gardener?' asked the stranger, intrigued.

'The truth is that all men are like the dance and light emitted by a lit fireplace in a dark room. The flames lift man to the heavens of his divine nature, while at the same time they create frightening, shapeless shadows on the walls of the room. This is the double nature that we all participate in; the two masks that we all wear in the theatre of life.'

The Mirror

One morning, while washing his face, the gardener stopped to stare at his image reflected in the mirror. And smiling he said to himself:

'Do you know something? I believe that in time I will end up becoming accustomed to your oddities.'

Insecurity

An extremely worried friend of the gardener was urging him to change his life.

'You can't live this way forever, you should come to your senses and think about getting a secure job. You're too old now to be playing about in life. You can't live with the uncertainty of not knowing if tomorrow you will have something to eat or not... '

'By the way,' the gardener interrupted. 'The other day your boss came to take a walk through the garden and I heard him say to the person who accompanied him that he wasn't very pleased with your work.'

A worried look appeared across the friend's face.

'What... ? Is this true?'

The gardener let out a chuckle at his prank, and said to his friend:

'Who's living in uncertainty?'

The Garland

Solitude reigned majestically in the depths of the garden, and the gardener, avid for the black silk of the star-covered sky, lay down on the soft grass of the summer night.

The peaceful sky looked for a place in his heart, and from there broke through his lips with a serene song of the Children of the Earth.

'Distant stars that reach my heart, lost in a corner of infinity; so close to me and so distant in your ignored beauty.

'If the wings of my spirit could lift my heavy mortal body, I would cross the sky to offer you my greetings one by one; and I would humbly ask that you grant me the gift of your gentle rays, so that with them I can make myself a garland of silver glinting lights.

'And I would keep it among my most loved flowers, waiting for the grand moment when Life calls me to cross the soundless gates of death.

'Then I would put it over my tired shoulders, and with it present myself before the King of the Universe. And I would say, "Lord, I have here the light of your presence in the darkness of my nights. I've braided it with the fingers of hope born from the echoes of your voice; and kept it like the bride's dress waiting

for the arrival of her beloved, to dress my bare soul on the day of our encounter. Do not ask me to shed it to see my heart, you know well that I am a child of the stars, and you will find in it only your own light in the darkness. Rather, let me bequeath myself to you in the final embrace, so that when I fade away in your breast, the heaven sings its rejoicing among a shower of stars."'

The Old Olive Tree

During a long walk through the hills, the gardener came across the recently cut stump of an old olive tree. Grieving over the lack of sensitivity of the tree's owner, capable of cutting off in an instant the life of a tree many centuries older than himself, the gardener sat down on a rock, remembering the powerful aspect of the tree, swaying in the wind with its silvery leaves.

Some time later he passed by that place again and found to his delight that new shoots had appeared from the sides of the stump, growing towards the sky with arrogant vigour. The gardener smiled, and mused about the arrogance of man, who sees himself as the owner of a world which doesn't belong to him; and over the bold defiance of life, capable of restoring itself time and again, contrary to the obstinate and malicious intentions of humans.

Stroking the tender shoots of the old olive, he whispered:

'There exists a stronger will than that of men.

'Who, old olive tree, can triumph over your willpower and desire to live?'

The Couple's Love

A man who had got married a few years back, was moaning to the gardener about the difficulties in his marriage.

In the beginning everything had gone well. For the first year after the wedding the couple had given each other all the love and sweetness that they had shared during their courtship. But, for no apparent reason, the relationship between the pair had later deteriorated to the point where the love they had once shared had changed into rejection and isolation.

'There are times when I think I hate her,' the man said to the gardener, 'and I think she hates me too.'

'How can love change to hate?' asked the gardener.

The man remained silent.

'Have you thought that the love you felt was not pure and true, but simply a feeling arising from mutual pleasure and recompense?' he asked again.

The man was looking down at the ground.

'In truth, I don't know now.'

The two men walked along the path lined with lime trees, on a carpet of red leaves which accompanied the silences of their conversation with its rustles. The gardener persisted with his questions.

'What were you looking for when you married her?'

'I was looking for happiness,' said the man resolutely, 'and I thought I could find it living with her.'

'There's your mistake,' said the gardener slowly. 'During the years you were betrothed to each other you took pleasure in everything together, and you had an ideal image of each other. You each thought that one person, with so many good qualities, could make you happy for the rest of your life. You didn't want to face the reality that, in front of you, was a person who not only had good qualities, but faults too. You didn't want to see the shadow.

'Over time, and by living together, that shadow appeared, and now you have put yourselves on the other side, where you only see the faults in each other and not the qualities.'

'Yes, something like that does seem to have happened to us,' said the man, dejected.

'Your mistake has been in each of you having looked for happiness outside yourself and not in your own hearts,' continued the gardener. 'If you had looked for happiness with the same feeling of love that filled your heart, your love would not have been dependent on your virtues or faults, but would have grown in understanding and affection towards the failures that, like all human beings, your partner has.

'And so, you would have mutually changed each other. Not through demands and blame, but through the love that was firmly installed in your heart.'

The man began to understand that perhaps there was a ray of hope for his situation.

'Then,' he said, 'what can I do now?'

'Look for happiness within yourself and don't hope that it is she who gives it to you, because you cannot ask anybody to give you what you yourself must acquire. Look for the love that you once felt in your heart, and find your pleasure only in that, and not in the love that she can feel for you. And absorb life through every pore of your skin, whether it is peaceful and happy or whether it is painful and sad, because in the total acceptance of life, with its magnificent days and its dark nights, one encounters the happiness that doesn't pass, the one that is in a safe haven, protected from storms and rough weather.'

'What you are saying isn't easy,' said the man with a sad smile.

The gardener stopped and regarded him sweetly.

'No, it isn't easy,' he answered serenely. 'And you will need the boldness of a warrior to reach the prize in the tournament of life.'

Happiness

'What must I do to discover happiness?' asked the beautiful young girl.

The gardener let out an innocent laugh.

'Don't look for it,' he replied.

The girl was confused.

'How can you say that?' she asked, somewhat irritated by his laughter. 'Everybody looks for happiness... '

'And very few find it... ' interrupted the gardener, still laughing.

The impulsive young girl began to get indignant, and this did nothing but increase the man's amusement.

'Look... ' continued the gardener, trying to calm her. 'Everybody is looking for happiness. Some look for it in the person they love, others in amassing money and goods, others in the attainment of their dreams... Everybody goes through life pursuing a dream, and when they succeed in attaining it, they experience a happiness which they believe will last forever. But, some time later, the monotony and the disappointment return, and everybody looks again for a new dream to make real, until they obtain it and then they again fall into disillusion, and so on.'

'You mean it's not possible to find lasting happiness?' the girl asked him again.

'Oh, no! I didn't mean to say that.'

'So, then, how does one obtain lasting happiness?' insisted the girl, visibly impatient.

The gardener made a gesture to her to calm down.

'It isn't obtained,' he answered. 'You cannot obtain something that has always been within you.'

'Gardener, you're going to drive me crazy. If I've always had it, how is it I don't feel it?'

'By any chance do you notice the flower you wear in your hair?' asked the gardener.

'When I stop to think about it, yes,' she answered, raising her hand to the flower.

'By any chance, don't you realize how happy you were when you stop to think about your past?'

'Well... Yes... ' she stuttered. 'But... '

'Well, stop to think about the happiness you feel now,' the gardener interrupted her. 'Everybody behaves like the man who spends the day looking for his glasses, to end up realizing that he has been wearing them all the time.

'We've always been happy, but we only realize it when time has elapsed and distance lets us see the entirety of the experience.

'Happiness has always been inside you, it has never left. Not even when life has made you go through pain and grief. You just didn't see it – your stubbornness to find it, and to run away from the hurt, has stopped you from seeing it.

'Pay attention to your life, to what surrounds you, to what you are feeling... and you will find that you are already happy. In that moment, happiness forms a part of you, because happiness is like a green meadow where life spins its dances of life and death, of love and solitude.'

And stroking the girl's cheek, he said sweetly:

'Don't look for happiness. If you want to look for something... look for life itself.'

The Sad Fairy

One midsummer's night, when even the inland wind did not allow the earth to cool down with the dew, the gardener came out of his hut with the intention of taking a bath. It was now very early morning, and after a lot of tossing and turning in his bed, trying unsuccessfully to get to sleep, the gardener decided to get up and go and cool down in the pond.

On the way, he was passing by a vast mass of primroses when he suddenly came upon a fairy sitting on a flower.

The gardener stopped to look at it, but the fairy did not seem to notice the man's presence. With her elbows on her knees, she kept her head rested between her hands, wearing the sad appearance of a small child.

'Good evening, small one,' the gardener said to her, causing the fairy such a start that she fell off the flower and disappeared in the foliage.

'I'm sorry I made you jump,' he said, when he saw her appear again amongst the leaves.

'Oh, don't worry, gardener,' the fairy said. 'It was my fault for not realizing your presence.'

And she sat on the same flower again, in the same position in which the gardener had found her.

'What's the matter with you?' he asked. 'You look sad and low.'

The fairy looked at him like someone who has come out of a dream, and took a while to answer.

'Oh... well... it's... I don't like being a fairy.'

'Why?' asked the gardener, surprised.

'Because I'd like to be clever like the gnomes... or intelligent like you human beings.'

The gardener considered the fairy's answer for a moment, at the end of which, he said:

'Intelligence is useful for some things, but not for others.'

'Why not? Intelligence is very useful for everything in life...'

'No, no, no!' the gardener interrupted. 'The most important thing is not to be intelligent but to be wise.'

'I don't understand,' the fairy said, moving her head.

The gardener sat down on the ground in front of the fairy.

'The oak tree is not intelligent but it is wise indeed, as it is capable of creating seeds full of life that the most intelligent man could not create.

'The eagle isn't intelligent, but it is wise; when rearing a chick, it knows exactly what it has to do in order that the chick grows healthy and becomes a majestic bird. However, there are many men who are intelligent but not wise; they are involved in feuds and wars, and they use their intelligence to discover ways to destroy and hurt other men.

'Don't confuse intelligence with wisdom, and don't wish for something that you don't need to carry out the mission that Life has entrusted to you. She gives to each one what is needed for them to do what has to be done, and she gives them wisdom within their own nature so that, without any effort, one can do whatever is necessary at the right moment.'

A beautiful smile was drawn on the fairy's face.

'I believe I understand you.'

The gardener softened his voice, and with words full of tenderness, he said to her:

'Don't wish to be anything other than what you are, a delicate and beautiful fairy. Because with your beauty you fill the woods with enchantment and joy, and with your wisdom you scatter the land with the colours of the flowers and the fragrance of the aromatic plants.

'What would become of us men without the sweetness of your work? What do we want so much intelligence for, if we are not capable of giving a flower its fragrance or the deep wood its imperceptible magic?'

And the fairy, jumping for joy, flew quickly towards the gardener's face, giving him a kiss on the tip of his nose before disappearing swiftly among the branches of some nearby cedars.

The following day, once more, the neighbours of the village wondered what had happened to the gardener's nose, to make it shine with such a golden brilliance.

Silence

Nobody knew what had happened to the gardener. For a week nobody saw his lips move, and when his friends asked him the reason for his silence he simply smiled at them and raised his shoulders in a resigned gesture.

In the village some said he had lost his voice, others said that God had left him mute in order to prevent him from spreading evil with his words, while others said that he was crazy and this would be another of his absurdities.

At the end of ten days he spoke again, and when a friend asked the reason for the long silence, he told him:

'In the last few months my lips have spoken too many words to too many people, and at times like these you run the risk of your words becoming empty of wisdom like the shells on a beach - although they can appear beautiful, they have neither soul nor life. That's why my mouth has remained closed, resting in the silence of the Spirit; because it is from silence that the word that nourishes and feeds emerges.'

The White Plain

During those days, the gardener prayed in the silence of his soul:

'Do not let my golden chant become clouded with the dark thoughts of a gloomy morning. Nor let go of my child-like hand in the middle of this silent desert. Although the smiling moon is with me in the solitude of my heart, my captive soul waits the blinding twinkle of your eyes.

'Do not forget the promises you made, when from a futile dream you came to wake me with a kiss. It isn't only the blood of my soul that I offered you in the repository of my hopes, now lost in the memory of the certain twilight.

'Don't stray from me, don't hide from my heart.

'Don't let the crystal flowers of my crying be lost in the sands of the past.

'Like iced frost on the windows in winter, my love waits for your tender call, clinging to the glass of the roaming future, trying to catch a glimpse of the sweetness of your presence.

'Listen to me. Turn your luminous face to me again. Look me in the eyes with that sweet look of yours. And tell me that you are waiting for me on the white plain, to take me in your hands to the altar in the temple of sacrifices.'

Blessed

The powerful storm clouds were moving away from the hardy inland regions, and through the chinks of their dark mass, the sun returned again to its task.

Suddenly, a ray of sun hit the steep slope of the path on which the gardener was walking, inhaling the scent of the humid earth, and the figure of a small snail stood out, slowly dragging itself among the herbs.

The gardener stopped and contemplated it for a long while, at the end of which he said:

'Blessed are the slow, because they don't miss even the smallest detail of life.'

The Master

It happened during the first days of summer.

An elderly foreigner, tall with blue eyes, appeared in the village asking for the gardener. When the two men met they joined in a silent embrace, and the gardener, with the best of his smiles, invited him to stay in his cabin.

The man was there for five days, and the people of the village saw them pass through their streets and along the paths of the area, absorbed in long conversations. Some said they had seen them talking until the early hours of the morning at the door of the hut, and all the while the gardener treated the elder man with respect and reverence.

At the end of that time the foreigner left, saying good-bye to the gardener with tears in his eyes. The two men knew that they would not see each other again in mortal flesh, but neither of them could admit what they knew in their hearts.

During the following days the gardener was silent and sullen, and nobody dared to ask about the strange man who had stayed in his hut.

Finally, one morning, one of his friends plucked up the courage to ask about the elderly foreigner.

'That man was my master,' the gardener admitted, 'and that is why you saw me treat him with such respect.

'Many years ago he showed me the way that my eyes failed to succeed in finding, he prepared my heart and my intelligence to face up to the dangers and difficulties I was probably going to find on the way, and he gave me the strength and determination of a warrior so I could manage to get to the end of the task I had undertaken.

'He showed me the way, but he didn't walk it for me. He taught me to stand on my own two feet without needing more help than that of Life itself pounding inside my heart. He educated me in the ethereal kingdoms of the Spirit so that I could speak face to face with the invisible forces of earth and heaven. And he fed me with his love so that I could grow free and self-reliant.

'But the most sublime gift that he could give me, that elder, was the example of his presence, his way in life, tender and strong at the same time, sweet and severe in his judgement, defiant before the storms of destiny and death.'

The gardener, moved, pressed his lips together while two large tears trickled down his face.

'This has been our last meeting,' he said serenely. 'His soul is prepared for the last flight ... that which will take him to the sacred mountain of Light ... to the golden palace of the Chosen.'

Beneath the Moonlight

It was a simple dream, but it would stay in the gardener's heart for the rest of his life.

He dreamt that he was in his garden, looking up at the Moon, listening to the songs of the crickets. Suddenly, he saw his soul rise, evaporating, up through the sky towards the moon's round ivory face. From the sky he saw his hut and his garden, and then the village and the surrounding area, and he recognized places where he used to walk and the houses where his friends lived, where the dogs acknowledged him with their barks.

He kept on rising until the sun peeped out from behind the earth, with a burst of light which, however, did not hurt his eyes. Then he realized that he was encircled by the black velvet of an eternal night, in which the sun shone with an incredible splendour. It was very strange for him to be simultaneously half in the brightest of day, and half in the darkest of nights.

When he arrived on the Moon he could not keep his eyes off the Earth, a precious half-blue Earth, floating in the blackness of a universe that seemed to pulsate.

His heart was stirred.

And with the eyes of his soul, he saw the absurdity of the poverty with which men on Earth covered themselves, the foolishness of their hate and war, the nonsense of their greed, envy, vengeance and lies, the stupidity of the borders and kingdoms of the world... And his heart grew with an overwhelming passion of love for the Earth, the origin of his existence, the loving mother who had fed and caressed him.

'Mother... ' whispered his lips time and again to the light of the Earth.

'Mother... ' whispered his lips when he awoke beneath the moonlight.

The Immutable Perfection

'The seed of wisdom is ignorance. When a man finds his ignorance he has just stepped into the threshold of the kingdom of wisdom.'

The gardener had said this with a faint smile, thinking that the group of youngsters who had come looking for his pronouncements would now be tired of so much conversation and would wish to walk through the garden.

But he was wrong. The youngsters did not seem willing to go without drinking something more from the fountain of his soul.

'What is the seed of happiness, gardener?' asked a young girl.

'Pain,' the gardener answered plainly.

'And of joy?' asked another.

'Sadness.'

'And what is the most perfect action?'

'The one that comes from absolute stillness.'

'And the origin of life?'

'Death.'

Silence hovered on the gardener's last word. Confusion was reflected on some faces, and on others doubt. The man lowered his look to the ground, and later, looking them in the eyes, said:

'Don't find what you have just heard from my lips strange, since true happiness can only be born from a profound understanding of pain and its causes; and true joy can only grow in the heart that has known the dark night of sadness.

'The most perfect action is that born from total stillness, for only in the stillness of meditation can man know the reasons for his movements, and the origin of life can only be found in freely accepting the death of the old, previously unsatisfactory existence.

'See how the seed must cease to be a seed if it is to become a leafy tree, and when it begins to extend its shoots it will need to feed its tender growing life from the decomposed remains of the dead leaves.

'See how the tide needs the ebb of the wave to gain its momentum and hurl again as a new wave that goes beyond the one before.

'See how nature needs the winter's rest to recover enough energy to radiate later in the height of summer.

'There is not Evil but Good in the course of growth, Good that hasn't yet reached its culmination. And death is nothing but the step to a new life that will reach its culmination, and with it the way to a new death that leads to a new resurrection.

'Life, the Universe, the Almighty, is in constant change, in a state of perpetual evolution between two poles that lead to a growing perfection. And from that constant change is derived the Immutable Perfection, like the incessant comings and goings of the pendulum, born from the fixed point from where the weight is hung.

'My words are strange only to anyone who still hasn't submerged himself in the paradox of life, the paradox in which the entire meaning and meaninglessness of Existence is found, where time stands still, where the Sun, the Moon and the stars stop in the sky, where all beings and the whole of nature stay silent...'

The Irresistible Wish

One warm Spring afternoon, the gardener felt full of energy. He had left his hut with the intention of meditating at the foot of the great evergreen oak, but when he got there he could not resist the temptation to climb up its stout branches.

After asking the tree's permission, he climbed up its trunk and immersed himself in the foliage of its leaves. When he was about to settle on one of the perches of the branches, he found that not more than a metre away was a small elf, looking at him with his mischievous eyes.

'Hello!' said the gardener.

'Hello!' the elf answered him. 'What are you doing here?'

The gardener shrugged his shoulders and said:

'Well... I felt an irresistible desire to climb up and... here I am. And you, what are you doing here?'

'The same as you,' the elf answered with a childlike gesture. 'I felt an irresistible desire to climb up and... here I am.'

'Oh!' exclaimed the gardener, moving his head.

And they said nothing more to each other.

The gardener sat at the point where the two branches met and remained silent, and after some minutes, the elf, without a word, climbed along his arm and sat down on one of the gardener's shoulders.

And the two friends contemplated the sunset through a hole that opened out in the thickness of the evergreen oak.

When the Fruit is Ripe

Sitting on the well-stones next to the apricot tree, the beautiful young girl and the gardener spoke about a mutual friend, while the man calmly ate the tree's fruit.

'I got to love him like I had never loved anybody before,' said the woman, 'but he took advantage of my feelings and made me believe that he too loved me.'

The gardener offered the girl a piece of fruit, but she silently refused it.

'How can you know how the fruit tastes without having gone beyond its skin?' the gardener asked her. 'Perhaps its flavour is sweeter than you think... Perhaps, simply, you haven't been able to understand how to appreciate the only thing he could offer you... '

The girl, feeling disillusioned, was not listening.

'I will never forgive what he did to me!' she said eventually, with the fire that blazed in her heart.

The gardener stroked her hair, and showed her the fruit which he had just opened saying:

'Did you see? When the fruit is ripe it comes away cleanly from the stone.'

The Monotonous Shadow

The gardener was returning to his hut after a morning's work in the garden when he suddenly stopped to observe his shadow that, lying down on the floor, seemed to look up at him with reluctance.

The gardener raised an arm and the shadow imitated his movement. Next, he raised a leg and shook it in the air and the shadow, faithful to its role, repeated exactly the same actions.

Lowering his arm and leg again, the gardener continued watching his shadow, and a few moments later said to it:

'You could surprise me any day now!'

The Harvest

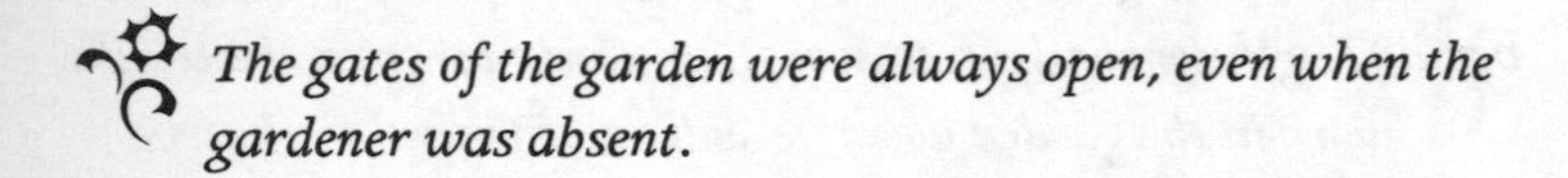

The gates of the garden were always open, even when the gardener was absent.

One of his friends, and a neighbour from the village, who had not had many dealings with him, had gone to his hut, and not finding him there decided to take a walk among the roses while awaiting his arrival.

'I can't quite understand this man,' said the neighbour to the gardener's friend. 'He could live much better than he does if he didn't scorn money so much. I don't doubt that he's an intelligent person who could give a good account of himself in whatever job he undertook. However, there you have him, living in that small hut with just enough to survive.'

'He doesn't understand life like we do,' the other said, defending his friend.

'But is there by any chance another way of understanding life?' the neighbour replied, sceptical. 'There's only one way to understand things in this world: the more money and the more possessions you have, the better. And if someone crosses your path to keep you from getting them, cast him out, quickly.'

The gardener's friend smiled.

'The gardener says that the plants and trees talk to men about life, and they do it with silent but wise words.

'He says that he who desires many things is like the tree that tries to load itself with too much fruit, so that come harvest time, it hasn't managed to ripen even one of them, and under the excessive weight of the unripe fruit, its branches end up bending to the ground, or, at worst, breaking off from the trunk.

'He says that, just as the farm-hand prunes the trees, man must shed his branches of unnecessary desires while he still has time, in order that when harvest time arrives he can give sweet and juicy fruit in abundance.'

With a wrinkled frown, the other man lingered a moment, thinking about the words of the gardener's friend. Eventually he asked:

'And what does your friend mean when he talks of this harvest?'

'He refers to the moment in which the soul of each one takes stock of his achievements in the life that was given to him,' was the answer.

'Then he mustn't cross my path,' the man exclaimed in a harsh tone.

And turning around he left without waiting for the gardener to return.

Daybreak

In the tranquil hours that precede daybreak the gardener left his hut, and took the path that rose from the ravine of red soil to the mountain. When the first light appeared on the horizon he sat down on top of a cliff, his soul pacified by the grand majesty of the landscape that began to stretch itself out to the timid songs of the birds.

The sun appeared in the distance.

The gardener, intoxicated by the air and light, closed his eyes. In his soul one hundred thousand poets chanted their verses, poets who from the distant dawning of life had bled their touched hearts in the face of the golden ecstasy of the dawn.

'Light...'

'Life... '

'Awaken... '

The gardener, in a very low voice, as if in an offering, started to sing.

The Nightingale

With the first heat of summer, a nightingale looked for shelter in the depths of the garden. From an old black pine tree beside the pond, it could be heard singing every night, pouring out its sweet melodies above the harmonic chorus of the crickets.

Ever since he had heard its voice the first time, the gardener had come every night to listen to its agile trills from the rocks of the pond. And there, more than once, he had found a young girl with blonde plaited hair, who had taken advantage of the carelessness of her parents during their entertaining nightly chats at the door of the house, and slipped away among the shadows of the street, looking for the garden's path.

On one of those nights, when the girl was listening enraptured to the bird's songs, the gardener appeared and sat down silently beside her.

'I have never heard anything so beautiful before!' said the girl, quietly, continuing to look in the direction from which the melody came.

The man smiled at the innocence of the girl.

'Perhaps that is why the nightingales sing at night,' he said in a whisper, 'so that we may appreciate the brilliance of their beauty without the songs of other birds to distract us.'

The girl turned towards the man, and with eyes wide open, she asked him:

'Gardener, have you ever seen the nightingale?'

'Oh, yes!' he answered. 'Yesterday afternoon I saw it flying about among the lower branches of the black pine tree.'

'It must be very beautiful if it sings those songs so prettily... '

'Oh, don't believe it!' said the gardener with a smile. 'It isn't much different from any other bird you already know. It's like a sparrow, but a little bigger.'

'But how can it sing so well without having vivid colours and a crest on its head?' she asked, intrigued.

'Because Life wants the best of essences to hide in the simplest forms.'

The girl looked with inquisitive eyes, waiting for an answer that her young mind could understand.

'Oh!... I'm sorry!' said the gardener, realizing. 'Look at the roses, the lavender, the jasmine... Where will you find more beauty and more perfumed aromas? If Life had wanted to give these flowers a more ostentatious setting he would have made them grow on trees with massive trunks that could be seen from the distance. However, they grow on humble plants with fine

stems, and they offer themselves at the height of our eyes and hands.

'Look at the bees, so small and humble by the side of the imperious eagle. Yet nothing can compare with the sweetness of their honey. It's in the small, the humble and the simple that Life has placed the image of her Soul.'

The girl, moving her head, showed the gardener that she was beginning to understand.

'I'm small,' she said. 'Do you mean that I am like the nightingale?'

'Yes,' answered the man, 'like the nightingale, like the roses, like the jasmine and the bees... '

'And when I get older, what will happen?'

'When you get older you will still have the image of the Soul of Life inside you, because in a human being's humble and simple shape She also put the essence of the universe.

'The divine presence is hidden in all human beings, but not all men sing forth their joyful hymns. Only a few, like the nightingale among the other birds, seek the night and the silence of its soul to open their hearts to the celestial melodies.'

'I haven't really understood what you're saying,' said the girl, lowering her eyes, 'but I suppose what I have to do is carry on being small, no?'

The gardener was touched in his heart by the wise innocence of the girl.

'Yes. You must stay small... ' he said in a whisper, '...and simple like the nightingale.'

Life

'Why are you always talking about life?' a friend asked him.

'Because it is that which we all have in abundance,' answered the gardener.

'Yes, but it isn't necessary to remind anyone that he is still alive.'

'Are you sure?'

'Of course!'

The gardener displayed a sly smile.

'Repeat that next time the tax collector comes!'

Incoherence

On one occasion, a young potter, greedy for the teachings of the gardener, asked him:

'Gardener, is there any harm that the soul cannot heal on the path to Life?'

The gardener raised his eyebrows with an expression of resignation.

'Yes, there is one.'

'And what is that?' the boy asked again.

'Incoherence,' the gardener answered plainly.

'Incoherence?' The boy was amazed, he had expected something more dramatic.

Moving his head, the gardener let out a tired smile.

'Incoherence is the tireless companion of the tireless searcher,' he said. 'It is the uninvited guest at the party, who ends up embarrassing you after having satisfied his appetite.

'The soul tells you which path you must take, and you accept in your heart that it is the appropriate one. But later - you do not know how - you see yourself walking along the wrong path without knowing how to explain to yourself what happened.

'One says this or that, and a little later one betrays oneself by doing the opposite, and the more the intention is formed not to fall, the more you make the same mistake.

'It's like an impertinent flea, in that the more you scratch the more it itches you.'

The youngster was trying to assimilate what seemed to be the enormous difficulty of being coherent about what one solemnly declares.

'Then, there is no way to achieve coherence between what one says and what one does?' he asked.

'It is possible to achieve a certain measure of agreement, provided that you don't begin to fight to the death with it, provided that you let it live beside you like a shadow that you can't detach from your feet.

'And when, finally, you make friends with your own incoherence, then it gives you a present that you weren't waiting for.'

'What?' asked the youngster, intrigued.

'Humility.'

The Poplar and The Oak

A young fifteen-year-old began to work with the gardener, looking after the flowers and trees in the garden. His father, an old friend of the gardener's, had asked him to take the boy in his charge, to teach him the craft that he knew so well, with the purpose of one day being able to do something to earn himself a living.

The boy, good-natured but as impatient as a hungry sparrow, did the work that the gardener asked of him with amazing speed, but without taking any care.

During his first days with the gardener, on one occasion, in his hurry he planted a cypress bush badly. The man called this to his attention with a severe frown:

'You must learn the lesson of the poplar and the oak,' he said severely.

The boy kept silent, waiting to hear the tedious recitation of the announced lecture. But seeing that the gardener did not start to speak, the silence weighed heavily, and he asked him, shyly:

'And what is that lesson?'

The gardener could not feign his annoyance any longer and burst out in resounding laughter, while the boy, quite confused, tried to force a smile. The man took the boy by the shoulders and asked him to accompany him.

'Leave your tools there,' he said. 'We're going to take a walk.'

And both of them left the garden, taking the path through the village that led to the river, until they reached the shore in the place where the ruins of the old windmill stood.

'Look, can you see that poplar?' the gardener said, pointing to a tall, slender tree.

'Yes,' the boy answered.

'And now, can you see this oak?' he asked again, showing him a young oak a little taller than themselves and with a trunk two fingers thick.

'Yes, why?' inquired the boy.

'These two trees are the same age,' the gardener declared emphatically.

The boy looked again at the two trees. He was surprised that the poplar was much taller than the oak and its trunk was twenty times as thick.

'But how can they be the same age?' he asked. 'The poplar is much bigger than the oak...'

'Yes,' the gardener interrupted him. 'It's much bigger because it grows much more quickly.'

The boy made a face that showed he was beginning to understand.

' ...but its wood,' the gardener continued, 'is not as good as the oak's.'

Silence.

The boy could not see what the gardener was getting at and he looked at him hoping that the man would continue.

And that is what happened.

'You want to do things too quickly,' he said to him deliberately, 'and you want to learn too many things in a short time. Just like the poplar, you are impatient.

'However, study the oak and learn from it. The oak takes more than forty years to become an adult, and even then it needs many more to acquire a thick and robust trunk. But its wood is the hardest and most resistant that you can find in the area, a wood you can use not only to make furniture, but also to make main beams that support the weight of houses.'

The gardener put his hand on the boy's shoulder, and kindly, and with a lot of tenderness, continued:

'This is what I wanted you to learn. If you wish eventually to make it as a gardener, you will have to learn to master the fine art of patience, because a gardener without patience will want

the trees and plants to grow in a few days, and that is a luxury that nature does not allow us.

'So, observe the oak well and imitate its calmness, so that eventually you yourself can be made of solid stuff with which you can build a house for yourself... and for all those who through your life ask you for shelter.'

And after that they kept on walking by the shore of the river, talking about the wisdom of the plants and leaving the work for a better moment.

Memories

The gardener was returning from working in a vineyard that he had bought on the outskirts of the village, when he stopped at the inn on the path that led to the town, which supplied provisions and shelter to travellers.

After asking the innkeeper for a glass of wine he sat down at an old solid oak table, at which a stranger was showing the first signs of drunkenness.

The man immediately assaulted the gardener with a trivial conversation about the severity of the weather in the region through which he had been travelling these last few days. There was no doubt that the stranger longed to talk to somebody, but the gardener, due to the tasks of the vineyard, was very tired and could not find too many words to offer him.

'Life is boring and monotonous,' said the man, looking at the glass of wine he held between his hands. 'Every day the same thing, one year after another... '

The gardener looked at him but said nothing. He also looked down at his glass of wine and thought that the stranger was wrong.

'Where is the fun in life?' continued the stranger. 'Some day... a moment... but nothing more.'

The gardener did not want to raise his eyes from the intense dark redness of the wine.

'Life!' he thought to himself. 'So full of mystery! So full of wonder!'

Many years of enchantment and hope began to pass through his mind, memories which he only shared with his closest friends; that mysterious past which enveloped the gardener's life, before his arrival in the village.

He remembered how everything had started, after an uneasy youth full of fascinating experiences. He remembered the voice which he had heard in his heart calling him to a destiny which he had not yet caught a glimpse of; and how he cried inconsolably at the edge of the path, due to the strong impression that the voice in his heart caused him.

He remembered those first years with a small group of friends, fervent worshippers of Life, lost in the mountains in long conversations with the forces of nature. He remembered the prophecies obtained from various strange people, speaking to them of a future hope that in the long search was always distant.

He remembered his master, that tall northerner with blue eyes, and his amazing spiritual teachings. He remembered the day he embraced the Light on top of the mountain and all those times he had sat down possessed by the Spirit of Life, while the peace that went beyond all comprehension immersed him in heavenly resting places.

He remembered his loves and his disappointments, his conquests and his failures, his superhuman efforts to reach the origin of Truth. He remembered those who on his travels had appeared with a big generous heart, to later disappear into the distant mist; and, also, those first young souls who had listened to his words with their hope resting in a better world; and he remembered that strange priestess of ancient cults who unintentionally plunged him into a sea of confusion and gave him the prodigious necklace which, ever since, he had kept as a symbol of his unattainable spirit.

He remembered his exile on the islands of the North, freely chosen and accepted, and his return to the bosom of his spiritual family, the marvellous adventure of friendship and the sour taste of separation.

And finally, he remembered his arrival in the village and the creation of the garden, after a prolonged abstinence in which he finally understood that everything was One.

There had been so many wonders, so many adventures, so many miracles...

How could that man say that life was boring and monotonous?

Perhaps his life had been, but there was no doubting that if that was so, it was probably because he had not dared to throw himself into the ocean of life with the boldness of one who speaks to God as an equal.

Or perhaps, simply, he did not want to accept that his life also had been marvellous.

The gardener came out of his dream of memories and noticed that the stranger continued with his long monologue about the tedium of life.

'Don't you believe it is so?' he asked the gardener finally, with the smell of wine on his breath.

The gardener smiled at him and said:

'No, my good man, I do not believe it is so.'

The Wisdom of the Trees

'What would the life of the tree be like?' the gardener's apprentice asked him one morning. 'What do they feel? How do they spend their time?'

'Do you truly want to know?' the gardener asked him.

'Oh, yes! I'd love to know.'

And the gardener made him stand motionless, absolutely still, in the middle of the wood, all morning.

When the boy returned to the hut at lunch time, the gardener asked:

'How are things? Do you know now how trees feel?'

And the apprentice replied:

'Yes... and I never thought I'd learn so many things in one morning.'

'You've begun to understand the wisdom of the trees,' the gardener said to him, satisfied.

The Wood

Among the irregular mountains that lay to the north of the village there was a silent lake that, from time to time, the gardener used to visit. It was a special and beautiful place, surrounded by woods and cliffs, from where the tranquil waters offered an intoxicating site of peace and beauty.

The gardener loved that place, and on many occasions he had sought its warm protection when doubt and confusion oppressed his thoughts. But the previous summer, a dreadful fire had razed to the ground the woods that he used to experience with such spiritual ecstasy. Saddened, the gardener had journeyed over the black slope of the mountain when the stumps of the trees were still smoking, and he had promised himself that he would return to give life to that desolate lake in so far as the strength of only one man was able to fulfil.

Just before winter arrived he had already covered the area with a bag full of seeds of maple and oak, placing the acorns as best he could in the damper places he found. And he continued his work sporadically all through that winter, hoping that the spring rain would give vigour to the seeds so that they would begin the path through life.

Shortly before the following summer he returned to visit the lake, searching among the new grass and the new growth of pines for signs of the life that he had sown. When he saw that among the shoots of rosemary there appeared the tender leaves of an oak whose seed he well remembered having planted, his joy was immense. He kept on walking and found more and more shoots of maple and oak, and the gardener reflected that his efforts that winter had been well worthwhile.

He then had a memory of the image of the first handful of seeds that he had taken from his bag, and the dreams that had left an impression on his hopeful mind as he grasped that handful of life between his hands.

In his imagination he had seen a deep, leafy wood, filled with trees with enormous trunks that covered the life that beat in the heart of the wood with a dense shadow. Aromatic plants, flowers, insects, birds, animals of every size were living under the shelter of that father wood, moist and nourishing, wise and responsible for the life it sheltered.

Now, he was seeing the first leaves of that giant wood emerging, a wood that he would never see in all its splendour, given that life was going to deny him the centuries that it generously offered to the trees.

But life, the gardener realized, had given him the possibility of entering into the fertile lands of eternity that crossed the wall of time... among the sweet mists of imagination.

The Other God

The gardener was having a glass of wine with a friend in the inn when from a nearby table he heard a man's voice rise up. This man had found himself passing through the village, and had struck up a conversation with some of the neighbours.

'God has been generous to me,' he said, with a certain amount of pride, 'because when I have asked for something, he has always granted it to me.

'Like you, I was a simple labourer. And tired of living with the uncertainty of losing the crop, I finally asked God to give me plenty of money and goods, so that I never had to worry about my sustenance.

'And God listened to me, and before a year had ended he gave me the opportunity to become rich, and I didn't waste it.'

During the comments of the customers of the inn, the gardener and his friend left to refresh themselves in the night breeze. Once outside, the friend asked the gardener his opinion about the traveller's words, and the man answered him:

'There is no doubt that this man was mistaken in his God.'

The Shortest Path

'Which is the shortest path to feel happy?' a man, wealthy and unaccustomed to work, asked the gardener.

'Always say thank you,' the gardener answered him.

'Always say thank you... to whom?' he asked again, confused.

'Always say thank you to Life for everything he gives us.'

The wealthy man smiled arrogantly.

'And doesn't it seem to you that if it was so easy, everybody would be happy?' he asked again.

'Oh, no! It's not easy!' answered the gardener. 'To be able to be thankful for even the pain that Life bequeaths us is not easy.'

The man stopped smiling when he saw what the gardener was getting at.

'Then, that can't be the shortest path... ' he said.

'Which is the shortest path to climb up the mountain?' the gardener then asked. 'Is it not across the land that leads directly from where you are to the top?'

'Yes, of course... '

'Is that path not,' the gardener continued, 'more difficult to cover than the path that snakes and goes up the mountain little by little?'

'Well... Yes, but... '

'The shortest path is always the most difficult and only the strong and brave can traverse it.'

The Hunt

The late summer heat was making itself felt across the land of the area, while the excessive evaporation of water had formed thick, dark clouds that threatened to unload a storm from the East.

Inside his hut, the gardener was busy catching flies that, as often happens some time before a storm, were being too bothersome and sticky.

At that awkward moment, a friend arrived and surprised him in the arduous hunting task he had undertaken. Thinking that the gardener was beginning to exceed the limits of what is thought of as acceptable for an 'eccentric' person, he asked him what he was doing.

'Hunting flies. Can't you see?' replied the gardener.

'Yes, of course I see that. But why are you hunting flies?'

'To make them fly outside the hut,' he said, without ceasing to chase his quick preys.

His friend made a gesture of incomprehension.

'But why don't you kill them?' he asked him. 'You will solve the problem sooner!'

The gardener stopped a moment, and smiling, answered:

'It's because... their time to die hasn't come yet.'

The friend was seriously starting to think that the gardener had gone crazy.

'And how do you know if their time to die has arrived or not?' he asked, losing his patience.

And the gardener, as if it was the most natural thing in the world, answered him calmly:

'It's very simple. If I can avoid them dying, then their moment to die has not yet arrived.'

And he carried on hunting flies.

The Sign

From a great mountain in the distance, he saw its powerful image coming, its strong wings moving with the elegance of one who knows he is lord of the sky, and when he reached the top of the garden trees he traced a large circle under the clouds.

For a long time, the gardener watched the eagle circling time and again over him. All through the morning his dance came and went across the sky, disappearing every so often only to return again, and scout the garden's surroundings.

Silence overcame the hidden life of the garden. The squirrels and sparrows could not be seen now; hidden, they had ceased their afternoon commotion. Only the soft rustling of the wind in the tree tops accompanied the mute figure that criss-crossed the air.

'Now I have understood your message, brother eagle,' said the gardener, observing the magnificent bird. 'You may return to your nest.'

And as if it had heard the man's words, the eagle lifted up in a sharp turn and disappeared in the direction of the mountain. It did not return.

The gardener had a saddened expression on his face. With his hands crossed behind his back and looking down at the floor, he moved away from the hut, little by little, along the path by the pond.

'Time is nearing its end... ' he said in a whisper to himself. 'The moment is coming... '

And he said nothing more.

The Language of Life

The gardener's apprentice had been working and learning in the garden some two years now. In that time he had become an amiable and responsible young boy, and to a great extent had grasped the crafts that the gardener had showed him.

But, suddenly, the gardener seemed to be in a hurry for the boy to learn all the skills that still needed to be learnt. He called him constantly to show him how to deal with this or that difficulty, and he encouraged him to practise what he was being shown as if the time between them was coming to an end.

'Why are you in such a hurry to show me everything I don't yet know about the plants?' he asked the gardener kindly, who looked at him with a sad smile.

'Don't ask what it is not yet time to answer,' the gardener replied with affection.

And after a short silence, he continued:

'However, it is time you were learning the Language of Life.'

'The Language of Life?' said the apprentice, intrigued. 'What's that?'

'It's the language that the world which surrounds you expresses itself in. The way the rest of the universe communicates with you.'

'I think I understand you,' said the young boy. 'With you I've learnt to read the trees and the flowers, to listen to the birds, to feel the insects, to discover the hidden lesson in everything that surrounds me.'

'But this is something else,' the gardener interrupted him.

And putting his thoughts in order to see how to explain it better, he continued:

'Sometimes, Nature, Life, tries to speak to you directly, to send you a message. Up to now you have learnt to listen to the voices of the beings that inhabit the world in which you're immersed, you've listened to their short stories, their wisdom, what they have learnt. Now you have to learn to decode the messages that Life sends to you directly, through them.'

The apprentice made an effort to understand the meaning of what the gardener was saying.

'And, how will I know that Life is trying to tell me something?' he asked, confused.

'You will simply know it,' the gardener answered him. 'There is something within everyone that lets them know that what has just happened means something, something important that one has to decode.

'Coincidences don't exist, and when something happens that calls our attention in that special way, it's because there's a message behind it.'

'And how does one read the message?' the youngster insisted.

'Not with your head,' said the gardener, 'but with your heart. The Language of Life is in some ways similar to the language of dreams. It speaks in images that make an impact on your heart, images that create clear sensations that allow your mind to open up to understanding. A stork gives the feeling of good news, of something about to be born; a wild boar promotes bravery and courage; a sudden storm carries away those already dead that are holding back the intentions of Life; a soft breeze that suddenly rises in the afternoon calm gives the sensation of a caress on being heard by heaven... When the heart is prepared to listen, nothing happens just because it feels like it.'

'I think I understand you,' the apprentice said, 'but, I would need time to be able to read clearly the Language of Life.'

The gardener looked at him with love in his eyes.

'You have got all the time in the world,' he said, finally. 'Make use of it. Open your heart to Life. Listen to it. And the messages will become clear to your soul under the pleasant robe of silence.'

The Pine on the Cliff

On the top of a high mountain cliff that looked spiritlessly to the lake, a twisted pine tree stuck its feeble branches out to the empty depths of the ravine that had been sculpted over the centuries by the river.

Whipped by the wind from the day it bore its first leaves, that aged tree clung to the earth and to life, its powerful roots penetrating the rock in search of the humid substratum which enabled it to keep on standing arrogantly facing the storms.

To the gardener, that pine tree was an image of the will to live, a natural symbol which was pleasing to watch when his strength grew weak in the face of the difficulties of existence.

On one of those days he went to visit it, on an afternoon when storms threatened. In the face of the strong wind and the galloping clouds, the old tree shook itself from one side to another, clinging tenaciously to its privileged viewpoint.

His hair loose in the wind, the gardener sat down on the cliff facing the tree. He studied it a long time, in its violent ritual dance for survival, until at last, impressed by its strength, he let his feelings flow from the depths of his soul.

'My brother, you have tempered your desire to offer your seeds to the wind, you have bent your wrinkled trunk in a thousand ways so that the storm doesn't tear off your branches. Tell me about the secret of your captive life, about the frailty of existence in your unyielding battle.

'Show me how you hardened your slender weak roots so that you could bite the painful rock of limitation, and tell me how to live within the emptiness of the uncertainty of our existence.

'Talk to me about the fierce storm of destiny, about the perpetual lashes of an unshared loneliness, so that I can accept the path that Life asks me for, as you accept your curious design.

'Share with me the views you have caught a glimpse of from your high vantage point. Speak to me about the serene majesty of the autumn rains on the lake, of the mysterious mists that winter moves to and fro over the water, of the scent of the mountains, of the tender dew... Remind my sleeping heart of the burning kiss of adventure and of love for the unknown, as Life asks me for one more jump into the void.'

The tears fell down his cheeks and were swept away by the impetuous wind. Getting up he approached the old tree, and in a warm embrace both of them hung over the abyss.

Children of Life

A woman from the city, a friend of the gardener's, went to visit him as the first September rains fell in the mountains. During the days she was in the garden she shared with the gardener and his friends the experiences she had undergone in the great prison in the city, where she used to go to generously lend her help to the prisoners.

The woman was full of energy and strength, convinced of the necessity of her work, which at times involved having to confront the politicians and the prison governors to obtain some advantage for the prisoners, or to get freedom for those who had been declared by doctors as hopeless cases.

When she left, a person from the village, who knew of the woman's stay in the hut and of her work in the city, said to the gardener:

'That friend of yours can't be in her right mind. Nobody thinks to help a criminal. How can there be someone who dedicates themselves to help those who are a danger to society?'

And the gardener told him:

'Doesn't it seem to you that, after all, they are the ones who need most help?'

'Well, no,' said the neighbour. 'They were able to choose their path and they chose the one that led them to ruin.'

The gardener shook his head.

'If one of your children chose the wrong path, wouldn't you try to help him so that he reformed and returned to the right path? Or, if you couldn't, wouldn't you ask one of his brothers to look after him?'

'Of course I would!' exclaimed the neighbour. 'But, those who are in prison are not my children...'

'They are the children of Life, like you and me,' the gardener interrupted. 'And Life cannot wish for anything more than that one of his brothers looks after them. People like that woman, who have the courage to give their care and affection to those who are rejected by the rest, are necessary. It's very easy to be charitable with those who touch our hearts; but it's very difficult to give the best of yourself to those who have lived in violence, resentment, hate and selfishness. Their path of commitment is the most difficult. And the most thankless, in that they must accept that others will reject their loving task.'

The neighbour refused to understand the gardener's explanation.

'I can accept that your friend is a kind-hearted person, in the same way as I think you are,' he said. 'But I still think that it is a mistake to help all those criminals.'

'My heart and that of my friend's are not any better than yours,' the gardener said to him sweetly, 'nor better than the hearts of those who are in prison.'

The Love of a Mother

The gardener was walking hurriedly to the hut. It was now more than an hour since he had left his meal to heat on the fire in the house, and he was afraid that his forgetfulness would cause him the inevitable inconvenience brought about on these occasions.

As he passed by the corner of a pile of small stones that lay beside the house, he tripped over and fell flat on the floor, as stretched out as his body would go.

He drew his battered body up onto his elbows, and with his face covered in dust, said:

'How much you love me, dear Mother Earth. As soon as you see that I put my feet in the air, you run to embrace me!'

The Gnome's Treasure

'What are you doing?' the gardener asked a gnome who was digging beside a large mushroom.

'I'm looking for treasure,' he answered, carrying on with the digging.

'I don't think you're going to find treasure there,' the man said to him. 'In this area there isn't any great wealth.'

'No! I'm not looking for wealth!' exclaimed the small being. 'I'm looking for my own treasure.'

The gardener tilted his head as dogs do when they hear something strange.

'And do you think your treasure is there?'

'It doesn't matter if it's here or not,' the gnome responded.

'Then why are you looking for treasure?'

The gnome stopped work, turned to the gardener with his hands on his waist, and showing signs of losing his patience, he said:

'Why do you think I'm looking for treasure?' And without waiting for an answer, he declared, 'To feel alive!'

And he continued shovelling while the gardener, a little baffled, chose to depart in silence.

Appreciation

In the course of a long conversation, the gardener said to a friend of his, who was a city bailiff:

'We should never wait for others to assess what we do.'

'No? And what would you do if suddenly somebody in the city had a party in your honour?' the bailiff asked him.

'I would say that they didn't know me, and if they truly knew me they wouldn't have a party in my honour.'

'And if they honoured you here, in the village, where they do know you?' his friend asked again.

'Then I would think I must be doing something wrong.'

Like a Child

The flowering jasmine spread its delightful perfume through the surroundings of the stream. Over the paved slopes at the foot of the jasmine, the gardener took pleasure in the intoxicating scent of some full-mooned, white lacquered flowers, while from his lips emerged a chant, spread by the warm breeze of the interior lands.

'For love of You I created this garden, and in its fragile flowers I placed the delicate kiss that as a lover I would have wanted to lay on Your soul. I thought that from Your distant throne You would see, lifted towards you, the green leaves that my hands nurtured, and is if they were my hands they would present to you a multi-coloured offering.

'My boldness was the simple act of a child who has fallen in love with one who cannot be reached even on the tip of one's toes, who courts and declares his love, and offers his sweets or coloured stones.

'What joy I would feel if you would just lay down Your look upon my hopeful hands and Your mouth would illuminate me with the light of Your smile!

'What joy if you accepted my lovesick flowers, and ran Your gentle hands through my hair as a caress!

'Like a child, I would consider myself satisfied with a jump of joy, and I would go to play along the path, crossing over your gardens, that lead to the forgotten lands.'

The Vision

The gardener submerged his soul in the oldest wood in the area. For three days he walked, wandering among the thick trunks of the trees, as naked as nature had first made him, sleeping among the bracken and mushrooms, and drinking only the crystal clear water of a murmuring stream.

Among the boxwood and the honeysuckle he sang his chants of praise, and under the solid rays that penetrated the depths of the wood he raised his hands to the sky, making an offer of his life and soul.

On a peaceful, late afternoon he heard his steps, light and faint, like the whisper of a breeze in the branches; and among the leaves of a holly tree he saw it appear, delicate and proud, beautiful and pure in the soft whiteness of its skin.

'The unicorn!' the gardener exclaimed in a low voice, opening his eyes in astonishment before the magnificent mystery.

Meekly, the beautiful animal approached him, and between tears of joy the gardener stroked his velvety neck.

The Gates of Mystery

And the unicorn opened the gates of the mystery for him, and carried him gently to the kingdom of Light from where he came.

From that day he understood the language of the birds, the conversations of the trees in the moonlit nights, and the stories that the water tells in the cascades.

And he understood that all Earth was his garden, the beloved present that Life gave him from the eternal night of his conception on the shores of time. And he knew that the stars shone for him, and the sun blazed for him, and that Eternal had kept a corner for him in the irremediable brilliance of Its blinding light.

For many nights he danced with joy in front of the fire, and called to his friends of the water and wind, and he shared his vision with them. And the elves and fairies saw him sing happily by the ravines, intoxicated in his merriment, and his illuminated soul swelled with Life.

And he cried out to the Sun and Moon, to Life and Death, among tears of joy...

'The dream has finished! ... The dream has finished!'

The Beaches of Eternity

'Gardener, what have you brought in your heart from the old wood? Your eyes speak of different worlds, and your silence rings in my heart with the echoes of a wedding feast.'

'From what I see, your soul is attentive to the trace that the marks of Eternity leave,' the gardener said to his apprentice. 'So it is right that I should speak to you of the exhilarated peacefulness that my heart embraces, of the reflection of eternity that Life has deposited in my eyes...

'In the old wood, the yearning that my injured soul has carefully searched for from the dawn of its existence, was fulfilled, and my hands were not my hands, and my lips stuttered the hymns of men in the bowels of the earth.

'In the old wood I came across the pure essence of the soul of Life, immaculate in its beauty, powerful in its white innocence; and it offered me its noble skin, so that with my caresses and through my hands, I discovered the eternal joy of the present and the gay triviality of actions and thoughts.

'There I knew the impassive joy of the righteous, and I drank from the sacred cup that hides the impurity of man. It is only offered to those relinquishing their life to go up to the altar of sacrifice, so that their blood feeds the holy universe.

'All the mysteries were revealed to me in an instant; every corner was illuminated with a great outburst of light which spread its rays to the remote parts of creation.

'The abundance of the Void... the conscious Uniqueness... the unique Life... useless and unnecessary... farcical in its absolute simplicity...

'And I felt the simple joy of a child, playing on the beaches of eternity by the murmuring sea of existence... lost in the boundless immensity that exists beyond time...

'God... One... Void... Existence... Life... Light... Beauty... Love!'

The gardener kept silent for a moment, lowering his head with a smile that revealed the peace that seized his heart.

'My lips are sealed when I try to express what only my soul has been able to taste in the profound delights of absolute peace.'

Something deep in the apprentice's soul understood.

The silence lay like a bridge between their hearts, and from the silence they conversed for the whole of that night.

When the rooster crowed, the apprentice's eyes were bathed in the sweet tears of he who has felt the powerful presence of Life.

The Time to Depart

The Spirit of the Wind went to visit him on the shore of the pond. A sudden gust, full of the dampness of the sea, played with the branches of the maple trees that not long ago had recovered their green robes.

'Peace to you gardener,' the Spirit greeted him politely. 'I've come to tell you that the moment to depart has now arrived.'

On hearing his words, the gardener's face, which had lit up on the arrival of his friend, was crossed by a sad shadow.

'The moment has arrived at last?' he said softly.

'Yes, my friend,' the Spirit of the Wind answered kindly. 'This time I wanted to come myself, instead of sending you my brother, the Spirit of the Eagle, again, because I knew that the news I bring you from the Greatest was going to make you sad.'

'I'm grateful to you,' the gardener said, looking at his blue celestial presence. 'And I'm grateful for the friendship that has bonded us together in the time we've spent here together, in these lands.'

He got up, shaking the dust from his clothes, and smiling again, he asked the Spirit of the Wind:

'Will you come with me on my long journey?'

The Spirit let out a burst of laughter.

'In which part of the Earth does the Wind not exist?' he said to him. 'Wherever we go, sooner or later we will meet, and we will have another fiesta like we had in the old wood.'

The two of them fell silent. The Spirit of the Wind saw the hurt in the gardener's heart, as he lowered his head and stared at his feet.

'You know... ? I'm going to miss these people,' the gardener said finally. 'I... '

He could not go on speaking. Two swollen tears rolled down his cheeks.

'Don't say anything,' his friend said, resting his hand on the gardener's shoulder.

'Wherever you are I will bring you news of these people, and cupped in my hands I'll bring you gentle breezes with the fragrance of these lands, the perfume of rosemary, thyme and lavender, the perfume of jasmine... '

The gardener interrupted him: 'Don't think I've lost my peace. Now, even sadness is a joy in the lap of my mother; Life. My heart is free of bonds and burdens, and I am prepared to set off for the distant horizon.

'They are just the tender shackles of love that are making my tears swell. Only his sweet embrace arouses my weeping.'

'Go, then, and say good-bye to everybody,' the Spirit of the Wind told him. 'Within three days I will send you the cold north breeze to join you in your departure.'

'As you wish,' answered the gardener.

And the Spirit of the Wind left towards the West, with an ache in his heart for his beloved friend.

Farewell to the Garden

For a whole day the gardener walked along his garden paths, saying good-bye to the trees and flowers, and lingering over his farewell among the foliage of his orchard.

He embraced the great oaks, so powerful and wise, and said farewell to the maples and the birch, the plane trees, the yews and the hawthorns; he sank his arms and body into the ivy and the honeysuckle, and he submerged his head in the Looking Glass Spring, pleading with it never to stop returning the image of its neighbours' eyes framed by the sky.

He breathed in for the last time the perfume of his jasmine and his roses, gave thanks for the simplicity of the verbenas and daisies, and placed a sweet kiss among the fairy primroses.

He refreshed his feet in the stream, asking it to strengthen him for the long journey that was about to begin, and he bathed his body in the pond, in a sacred baptism of initiation to the new life that had just begun.

And the irises and the camellias cried softly at his farewell, and the pansies kissed his feet as he passed along the garden path, and the trees, murmuring and sincere, stroked him with a shower of leaves.

How much were they loved! How many caresses had been lavished on them since the distant creation of the garden!

The gardener climbed on to the rock of the pond, and from there spoke to the trees and plants, to the birds and flowers, the squirrels and butterflies.

'Don't think I'm abandoning you - my place will be taken by one who, until now, has been my apprentice. Love him as you have loved me and talk to him as you did to me, so that the sweet nectar of your tenderness fills his empty steps.'

And when night arrived he invited his friends of the wood and flowers to a feast - the elves, the gnomes, the nymphs, the fairies and the mischievous imps. And he embraced them one by one, and he asked them not to abandon his garden, and to make themselves known to his apprentice, and to forgive man for his ignorance and arrogant pride.

The moon rose behind the mountains and the fairies went to sleep.

The gardener was alone, before his beloved pond ... with a golden brightness on his nose.

Towards the Distant Horizon

The breeze of the North arrived in the mild spring morning.

The gardener thanked his hut for its years of warm shelter, and crossing the door, bid farewell to his beloved small plant.

He tenderly embraced his apprentice and his friends from the neighbourhood, and from the peace of his heart, said to them:

'Other lands and other people, who from the heart of Life have persistently called me, await me. I leave you my love in the form of the garden, and a new gardener to cure your pains.

'And take care of what Life has given to you; your mountains and plains, your scarlet land and all the beings that live in them; make sure it is your greatest treasure and the face of God is always in your gaze.'

And with his long wooden oak stick and his leather sandals, the gardener set out across the red carpet of spring poppies, with the fresh breeze of the North... towards the distant horizon.